A Dragon on the Doorstep

written by Stella Blackstone

illustrated by Debbie Harter

There's a dragon on the doorstep,
Do you think he wants to play?

Let's lock him in the closet,
Then let's run away!

There's a crocodile in the closet,
Don't go inside!

Let's put him in the attic,
Then run downstairs and hide!

There's a spider in the attic,
Quick! Get out of here!

Let’s put him in the toy chest
And hope he’ll disappear!

There's a tiger in the toy chest
With a very fierce glare!

Let's chase him to the bedroom
And tell him to stay in there!

There's a big bear in the bedroom,
With the most enormous paws!

Let's hide him in the laundry
And make sure we shut the doors!

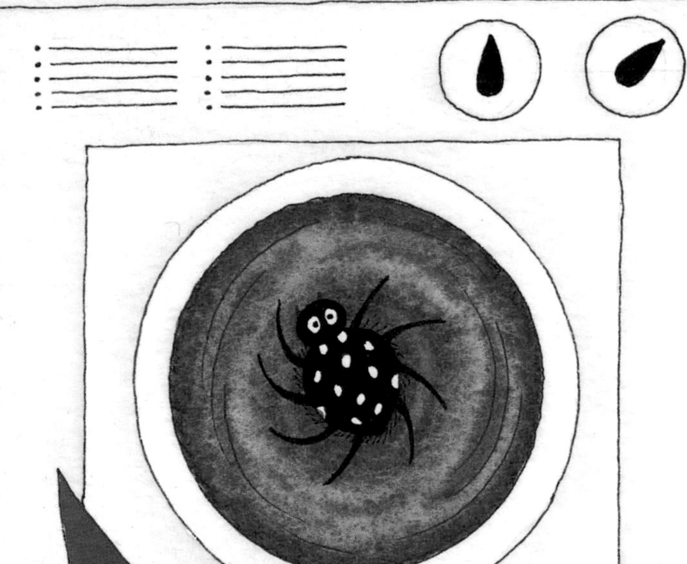

There's a lion in the laundry,
Have a look and see!

Let's shut him in the garage
And lock it with the key!

There's a gorilla in the garage
And all the others too!

Everybody has escaped!
Watch out or they'll catch you!

What a lot of animals!
Let's all go outside.

Then we can play another game
And everyone can hide!

For Sarah, with much love — S. B.
For Eva, Yoyo and Luke — D. H.

Barefoot Books
2067 Massachusetts Ave
Cambridge, MA 02140

First published in the United States of America in 2005 by Barefoot Books, Inc.
This paperback edition published in 2006

This book was typeset in Bokka and Mercurius Medium
The illustrations were prepared in watercolor, pen and ink and crayon on thick watercolor paper

Graphic design by Barefoot Books, Bath
Color separation by Grafiscan, Verona
Printed and bound by Printplus Ltd, China
This book has been printed on 100% acid-free paper

Paperback ISBN 1-905236-66-2

The Library of Congress cataloged the hardcover edition as follows:
Blackstone, Stella.
A dragon on the doorstep / written by Stella Blackstone ; illustrated by Debbie Harter.
p. cm.
Summary: Easy-to-read, rhyming text describes a game of hide-and-seek among the animals in a child's home.
ISBN 1-84148-227-7 (hardcover : alk. paper)
[1. Hide-and-seek--Fiction. 2. Animals--Fiction. 3. Stories in rhyme.] I. Harter, Debbie, ill. II. Title.

PZ8.3.B5735Dr 2005
[E]--dc22

5 7 9 8 6

2004028587